Learn
good habits
with
Jessica

My cousin Zoe eats candy—
a lot at a time.

Me, I'm careful about
what I eat.
I try to eat lots of fruits and
vegetables to be healthy.

Zoe goes to bed at midnight.

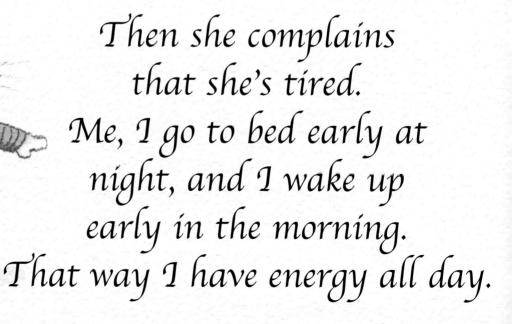

Then she complains that she's tired. Me, I go to bed early at night, and I wake up early in the morning. That way I have energy all day.

Zoe leaves objects lying around everywhere.

I put things away as soon as I'm finished with them. Plus I have to put her things away because she always makes a big mess when she visits.

Zoe throws food at me
when we eat together.

She thinks that's funny.
I never play with my food.
When a meal is ready, I sit
at the table and I eat
what's on my plate with
good manners.

Zoe's hands are always dirty.

My cousin doesn't know anything about being clean. Me, I wash my hands frequently, especially before each meal.

Zoe is always picking fights.

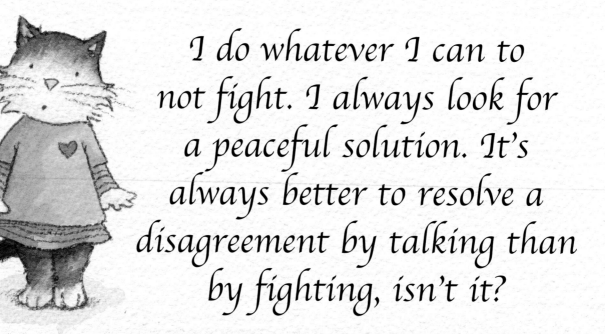

I do whatever I can to not fight. I always look for a peaceful solution. It's always better to resolve a disagreement by talking than by fighting, isn't it?

Zoe never turns off the lights.

I don't waste water or electricity. When I'm the last person to leave the room, I turn off the light. I'm also careful not to waste water.

When Zoe does something wrong, she always tries to blame someone else.

My cousin lies a lot.
Me, I never lie. I think being honest is very important.

Zoe has dirty teeth and bad breath.

Zoe doesn't brush her teeth very often. My teeth are clean because I brush them every morning and every night before I go to bed.

My cousin Zoe is very selfish.

*I think of others and their needs.
I always try to be helpful
whenever I can.*

Sometimes Zoe spends the whole
day in front of the television.

I like to watch television
also, but I'm sure not
to watch too much. I take
time to read and to talk
and play with my friends.

Zoe never lends anything to anybody.

I'm happy to lend my possessions to friends. I like to share. If you ask me, being generous is the best way to make friends.